MW01223192

972.910 Holland, G
HOL
        Cuba is my

DATE DUE	BORROWER	

972.910 Holland, Gini
HOL
        Cuba is my home

	DATE DUE		

My Home Country

CUBA
IS MY HOME

HERBERT SPENCER
ELEMENTARY SCHOOL
605 - SECOND STREET
NEW WESTMINSTER, B.C.
V3L 5R9

For a free color catalog describing Gareth Stevens' list of high-quality books, call 1-800-341-3569 (USA) or 1-800-461-9120 (Canada).

For their help in the preparation of *Cuba Is My Home*, the editors gratefully thank Professor Michael Fleet, Marquette University, Milwaukee; Professor Howard Handelman, University of Wisconsin-Milwaukee; and Lillian Rodriguez Kalyanaraman.

Library of Congress Cataloging-in-Publication Data

Holland, Gini.
    Cuba is my home : adapted from Ronnie Cummins' Children of the world--Cuba / by Gini Holland ; photographs by Mercedes Lopez.
        p. cm. -- (My home country)
    Includes bibliographical references and index.
    Summary: A look at the life of a twelve-year-old boy and his family living in Havana, Cuba. Includes a section with information on Cuba.
    ISBN 0-8368-0848-7
    1. Cuba--Social life and customs--Juvenile literature. [1. Family life--Cuba. 2. Cuba.] I. Lopez, Mercedes, 1961- ill. II. Cummins, Ronnie. Cuba. III. Title. IV. Series.
F1760.H65   1992
972.9106'4--dc20   92-17725

Edited, designed, and produced by

Gareth Stevens Publishing
1555 North RiverCenter Drive, Suite 201
Milwaukee, Wisconsin 53212, USA

Text, photographs, and format © 1992 by Gareth Stevens, Inc. First published in the United States and Canada in 1992 by Gareth Stevens, Inc. This U.S. edition is abridged from *Children of the World: Cuba*, © 1990 by Gareth Stevens, Inc., with text by Ronnie Cummins and photographs by Mercedes Lopez.

All rights reserved. No part of this book may be reproduced or used without permission in writing from Gareth Stevens, Inc.

Series editor: Beth Karpfinger
Cover design: Kristi Ludwig
Designer: Laurie Shock
Map design: Sheri Gibbs

Printed in the United States of America

1 2 3 4 5 6 7 8 9 96 95 94 93 92

My Home Country

CUBA
IS MY HOME

Adapted from Ronnie Cummins'
Children of the World: Cuba
by Gini Holland
Photographs by Mercedes Lopez

Gareth Stevens Publishing
MILWAUKEE

Twelve-year-old Alain lives in Havana, Cuba's capital city replete with historic buildings and a rich past. He practices hard at his fencing and harmonica and plays baseball, a favorite Cuban sport. Alain is fascinated by stories of distant countries and exciting times, and he listens eagerly to his father's tales of his world travels and his grandmother's accounts of her days as a guerrilla fighter during the Cuban revolution.

To enhance this book's value in libraries and classrooms, clear and simple reference sections include up-to-date information about Cuba's history, land and climate, people and language, education, and religion. *Cuba Is My Home* also features a large and colorful map, bibliography, glossary, simple index, and research topics and activity projects designed especially for young readers.

The living conditions and experiences of children in Cuba vary according to economic, environmental, and ethnic circumstances. The reference sections help bring to life for young readers the diversity and richness of the culture and heritage of Cuba. Of particular interest are discussions of the changes in Cuba since the revolution and its relationship with the United States and the former USSR.

My Home Country includes the following titles:

Canada	*Nicaragua*
Costa Rica	*Peru*
Cuba	*Poland*
El Salvador	*South Africa*
Guatemala	*Vietnam*
Ireland	*Zambia*

CONTENTS

Alain laughs with his mother, brother, grandmother, two aunts, and a family friend.

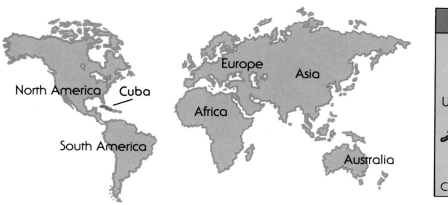

LIVING IN CUBA:
Alain, a Boy from Havana

Twelve-year-old Alain Alfonso Lamar thinks life in Havana, Cuba, is fun. He lives there in an apartment with his father, mother, brother, aunts, and grandmother. Alain's father, Alberto, works on an oil tanker out on the Caribbean Sea. Alain misses his father and is happy when the ship comes back to Havana.

Alain and his brother greet their father in front of the ship on which he works.

Alain's Neighborhood

The Spanish founded Havana in 1515. Now it has two million people. Alain's family lives in an apartment building built in the 1950s. Their neighborhood is much older. It is called Vedado, which means "forbidden," because the Spanish, who ruled Cuba from 1515 to 1898, would not allow slaves or poor people to live or even walk in this part of Havana.

Above: Alain looks over the movies listed outside one of the many movie theaters in his neighborhood.

From the top of his apartment building, Alain can see Havana's mix of old and new. ▶

Many tourists stay in hotels near Alain's home. His father's stories of faraway countries make Alain wonder about the lives that other people live. He wants to travel when he is old enough. For now, he reads about the world and plans to study English and Russian.

Buses are the main form of transportation in Havana.

Alain can see many hotels from his sixth-floor balcony.

Alain's family lives in a five-room apartment on the sixth floor. From the balcony of his apartment, Alain can look out over the entire neighborhood. He can even see the ocean if he leans out far enough.

11

Havana as seen from the top of a
hotel in the center of the city.

Daily Life in Havana

Alain usually wakes up about 7:00 a.m., makes his bed, and dresses for school. His mother, Xonia, has much to do before work, so Alain often cooks breakfast.

Sometimes Alain works on his stamp book before school. His father sends Alain stamps from all over the world. Alberto's work takes him to many different countries.

Left: Alain flips his egg with a steady hand.
A page from Alain's collection shows stamps of some of Cuba's popular sports. ▸

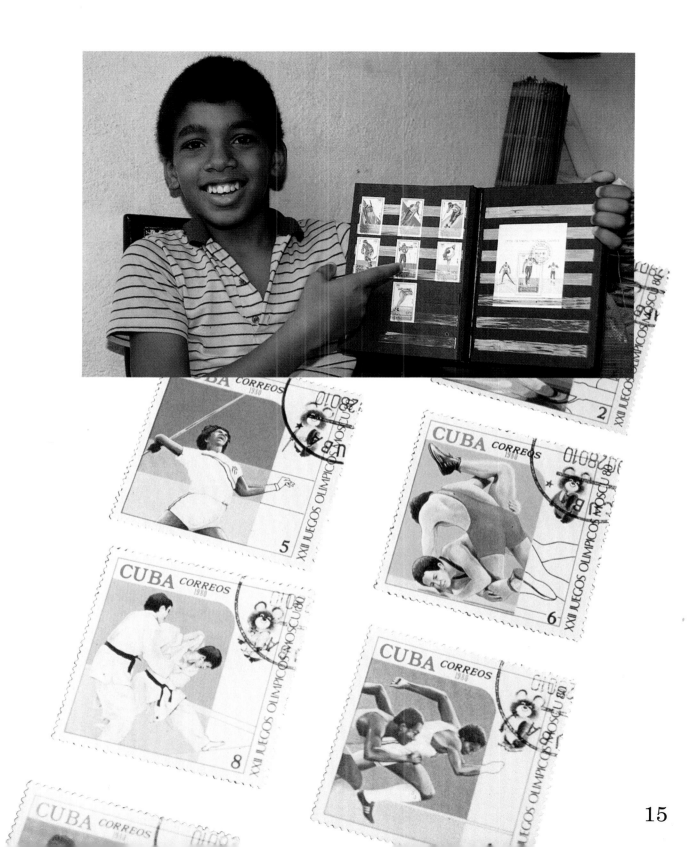

15

Before school, Alain, his aunt, and his mother often walk to the neighborhood market. The market carries food such as grains, milk, butter, vegetables, and canned goods. The government owns the store and helps pay part of the cost so that even poor families can have good food to eat. All Cuban families have a food card that shows how much food they can buy at the low price.

◀ **This small neighborhood store carries many basic foods.**
Below: Cubans bring milk bottles to the store to be refilled.

While Alain goes to school, his mother, Xonia, works as an accountant, his aunt Martha works for a video production company, and his brother, Alberto, works as an electrician.

Before school, Alain kisses his mother good-bye.

Alain's grandmother, Carlota, no longer works. Alain thinks no one would guess his grandmother is 56 years old or that, as a young mother, she fought with the rebel fighters in the mountains of Cuba. But her medals show that she was brave.

Alain's grandmother earned these medals fighting in the Cuban Revolution.

Alain's School

Alain walks to school each day. The Ruben Martinez Villena School is only three blocks from Alain's home. It is named for a Cuban revolutionary hero. Students wear uniforms, which are paid for by the government. Every grade has a different color uniform. Wearing the yellow and white uniform of the seventh grade this year, Alain feels very grown-up.

Alain stops to talk with a friend at the school gate. ▶
Alain walks to school with his best friend, Tony.

Cuban schools put science and math first, but they also teach reading, social studies, and the arts. Alain does well in all of these subjects. Before he graduates from school, Alain and his classmates must do public service, such as planting trees or helping out on farms. Alain hopes that his service will have something to do with science.

◄ **Alain stands with classmates in the school yard after classes. Below: Alain gets help with his homework.**

Alain Tours Old Havana

Alain wonders what it was like long ago, when pirates and soldiers fought in Old Havana. Between 1589 and 1630, the Spaniards built the Castle of the Moors after pirates attacked Havana. In 1844, the people of the city added a lighthouse. Alain's father always eagerly searches for the castle's light as his ship nears Havana Harbor.

Havana Harbor as seen from the Castle of the Moors.

Havana has two more castles. The Castle of the Point, with its thick stone walls and old cannons, is now a museum. The Castle of the Force is Cuba's oldest building. Alain knows that this castle was built in 1538 after other pirates attacked Havana. After they built the castles and forts, the Spaniards built the cathedral and other buildings of Old Havana.

Alain and his mother stand before a Spanish rug in the castle museum.

◀ **Alain and his mother stop at the Castle of the Point.**

Alain and his mother, Xonia, walk to Plaza de las Armas, where a tree marks the grave of Christopher Columbus. The Municipal Palace, built in 1776, stands near the plaza. Spanish presidents lived there until 1917, but now it is Havana's historical museum.

◀ Cuba's first Catholic mass took place beneath this tree.
Below: Alain looks at the old church bells from Havana Cathedral.

Two-fisted eating at the Coppelia Park ice cream shop!

After-school Snack

After school, Alain and his friends often stop in Coppelia Park, sometimes called the world's biggest ice-cream parlor. People crowd the park's tables and benches, eating every flavor of ice cream you can think of. Alain stands in line to buy ice cream for his friends. Like most Cubans, Alain often buys two cones at a time.

Alain can keep up with anyone when it comes to eating ice cream.

A 1950s Nash Rambler from Alain's neighborhood.

Havana's Cars

From his apartment, Alain watches cars moving below. He sees many are old US-made cars. After the Cuban revolution in 1960, the United States stopped trade with Cuba, so the Cubans can't get new cars from the United States. Now most new cars in Cuba are Soviet Ladas. Like most Cubans, Alain's family uses public transportation.

**Right: Cuba has many US cars
from the 1940s and 1950s.
Below: Alain would love a ride
in the sidecar of this motorcycle.**

Alain plays the harmonica for fun.

The Weekend at Last!

Alain takes it easy on weekends. He sleeps late and then watches television, reads, or listens to music. Often, he plays along on his harmonica. Sometimes, if he is too loud, Xonia asks him to practice in his bedroom or on the balcony.

Like nearly everyone else in Cuba, Alain loves baseball. Sometimes he even sees games in the Havana sports center. The weekend gives him lots of time for his sports. Besides baseball, Alain spends his free time lifting weights, playing basketball and soccer, and fencing, which is a kind of sword fighting.

Alain calls Tony about their baseball game.

A Day in the Park

Parque Lenin, Havana's largest park, is named after Vladimir Lenin, the Soviet leader. The park is very big, but a coal-powered train makes travel through the park easy. Today, as Alain and his aunt Xandra walk in the park, the train passes them, and the engineer toots his whistle. Everyone waves.

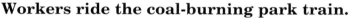

Workers ride the coal-burning park train.

Alain hurries Xandra on to the open-air theater. Climbing onto the stage, Alain pretends he is an actor. From the stage, he spots a group of school friends. They chase each other until Xandra calls Alain to get something to eat at the open-air market. Alain orders pizza and tamales. After lunch, they're off to the amusement park, where Alain rides every ride.

Top: Playing in the park makes Alain hungry.
Bottom: Schoolgirls drink water from a waterspout.

The Family Plays Together

Everyone in Alain's family loves to dance. When they're all at home, they often move the tables and chairs, put on a record, and dance. This afternoon, Alain can hear someone having a street dance. When his mother and aunts come home from work, Alain knows that they will want to join the street dancers.

Alain gets his mother dancing.

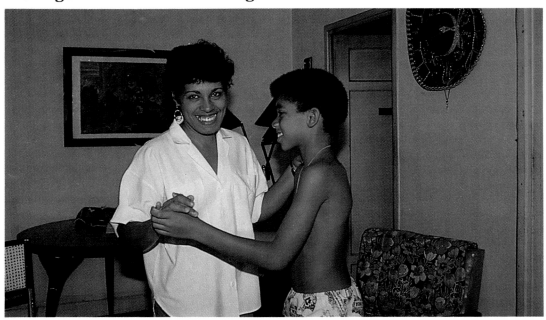

Wood carvings show African culture in Cuba.

An Afternoon at the Beach

On weekends, Alain and Xandra often hop on a city bus for an afternoon at one of Cuba's white sand beaches. Today, as a special treat, Alain gets to ride on a catamaran. As the boat cuts through the water, he feels the salty sea breezes racing past him. Alain remembers how his father says there is nothing quite like the ocean. Alain agrees.

Alain loves having the ocean as a playground.

41

MORE FACTS ABOUT: Cuba

Official Name: Republica de Cuba
(ray-POOH-blee-kah day
KOO-bah)
Republic of Cuba

Capital: Havana

History

The Siboneyes, Taínos, and Guanajatabeyes Indians
ruled Cuba until Christopher Columbus landed in
1492 and claimed Cuba for Spain. The Spanish
treated the Indians like slaves and eventually
the Indians were wiped out.

The Cubans fought the Spanish many times. The
rebellions were always put down, until finally, in
1898, the US declared war on Spain. The Spanish
soon gave up, and the Republic of Cuba was born on
May 20, 1902. The presidents who were in office
from 1902 to 1959 didn't give the Cuban people the
freedom they deserved. Finally, the Cuban people
decided to overthrow the dictator Fulgencio Batista.
Between 1953 and 1959, Fidel Castro led a fight
against Batista's dictatorship. Castro and his army
won on January 1, 1959. Castro's government took

control of all business and industry. Castro became friends with the leaders of what was then the Soviet Union, and brought Communism to Cuba. The US and many other countries did not like Communism. They stopped trading with Cuba. Many Cubans do not like living under Communism, and over one million people have left Cuba to live elsewhere.

Land and Climate

Just 90 miles (145 km) south of the US, Cuba is the largest island in the Caribbean. The main island is about 760 miles (1,220 km) long and 120 miles (190 km) wide. Cuba is a tropical island with much rainfall and rich farmland. Temperatures range from 71°-82°F (22°-28° C).

People and Language

Most of Cuba's 10.5 million people are of Spanish or mixed Spanish and African descent. Spanish is the official language. Cuba's native Indian population was wiped out as a result of the Spanish conquest.

Education

Because of the government's free education and students' good attendance, 90-95% of the people can read and write. Children get 12 years of primary and secondary school. Cuba has four universities and very good medical training programs.

Religion

The Cuban government says the Cuban people do not practice religion. But Cuba still has many Christians within its borders. In 1980, 39.6% of Cubans said they were Roman Catholics, and 5.3% said they had other religious beliefs.

Sports and Recreation

Baseball is the biggest sport in Cuba, but people also enjoy most other sports, including *jai alai*, a game like handball that came from Spain.

Cubans in North America

After the Cuban Revolution of 1959, 500,000 people left Cuba for Spain, the United States, and other countries. Today, over one million Cubans and people of Cuban origin live in North America. Most live in Miami.

Two twenty-peso notes and a one-peso coin.

Glossary of Useful Cuban (Spanish) Terms

barco (BAR-coh): boat

calle (KAH-yeh): street

castillo (kas-TEE-yoh): castle

escuela (es-KWAY-lah): school

playa (PLAH-yah): beach

More Books About Cuba

Cuba from Columbus to Castro. Williams and
McSweeney (Julian Messner)
Cuba in Pictures. Lerner Publications Dept.
of Geography Staff (Lerner)

Things To Do

1. Draw a map of Cuba showing where it is in the
world. Can you see its crocodile shape?

2. If you would like to have a Cuban pen pal, write
to these people: Worldwide Pen Friends, P.O. Box
39097, Downey, CA 90241.

Be sure to tell them what country you want your
pen pal to be from. Also include your full name,
age, and address.

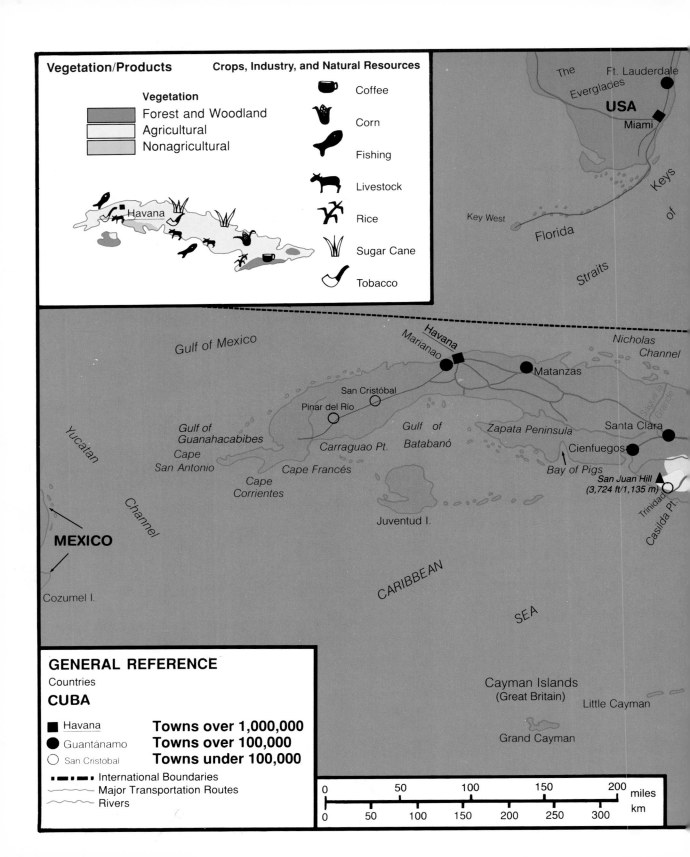

Vegetation/Products

Vegetation
Forest and Woodland
Agricultural
Nonagricultural

Havana

Crops, Industry, and Natural Resources

Coffee
Corn
Fishing
Livestock
Rice
Sugar Cane
Tobacco

The Everglades
Ft. Lauderdale
USA
Miami
Key West
Florida
Keys
of
Straits

Gulf of Mexico
Nicholas Channel
Havana
Marianao
Matanzas
San Cristóbal
Pinar del Río
Sagua la Grande
Santa Clara
Gulf of Guanahacabibes
Cape San Antonio
Carraguao Pt.
Cape Francés
Cape Corrientes
Gulf of Batabanó
Zapata Peninsula
Cienfuegos
Bay of Pigs
San Juan Hill (3,724 ft/1,135 m)
Trinidad
Casilda Pt.
Juventud I.

Yucatán
Channel
MEXICO
Cozumel I.

CARIBBEAN
SEA

Cayman Islands (Great Britain)
Little Cayman
Grand Cayman

GENERAL REFERENCE
Countries
CUBA

■ Havana   **Towns over 1,000,000**
● Guantánamo   **Towns over 100,000**
○ San Cristobal   **Towns under 100,000**

▪-▪-▪- International Boundaries
〜〜 Major Transportation Routes
〜〜 Rivers

0		50		100		150		200	miles
0	50	100	150	200	250	300			km

CUBA — Political and Physical

HEIGHT IN FEET AND METERS
feet   meters

6,000   2,000
3,000   1,000
1,000   300   Above Sea Level
0   0   Sea Level

Florida

Great

Sanataren Channel

Bahama

Bank

Nassau

Andros I.

Eleuthera I.

Cat I.

BAHAMAS

Tropic of Cancer

ATLANTIC

Crooked I.

Coco
Cay

Romano Cay

Old Bahama Channel

Arch. de Camagüey

Guajaba
Cay

Sabinal Cay

OCEAN

Jardines del Sur

Gulf of
Ana Maria

Florida

Camagüey

C U B A

San Pedro

Puerto Padre

Cape
Lucrecia

Nipe Bay

Holguín

Guarico Pt.

Jardines de la Reina

Gulf of
Guacanayabo

Bayamo

Cauto

*Sierra del
Cristal*

Manzanillo

Palma Soriano

Sierra Maestra

Turquino
6,561 ft/2,000 m

Guantánamo

Cape Maisí

Cape Cruz

Santiago de Cuba

Gran Piedra
3,710 ft/1,131 m

Guantánamo Bay
(U.S. Navy Base)

Passage

Windward

HAITI

Montego Bay

JAMAICA

Port-au-Prince

Index